"I was born in London in 1946 and grew up in a sweet shop in Essex. For several years I worked as a graphic designer, but in 1980 I decided to concentrate on writing and illustrating books for children.

My wife, Annette, and I have two grown-up children, Ben and Amanda, and we have put down roots in Suffolk.

I haven't recently counted how many books there are with my name on the cover but Percy the Park Keeper accounts for a good many of them. I'm reliably informed that they have sold more than three million copies. Hooray!

I didn't realise this when I invented Percy, but I can now see that he's very like my mum's dad, my grandpa. I even have a picture of him giving a ride to my brother and me in his old home-made wooden wheelbarrow!"

NICK BUTTERWORTH

Percy's Friends
The Rabbits

Nick Butterworth

HarperCollins *Children's Books*

Thanks Graham Daldry. You're a wizard.

Thanks Atholl McDonald. You're a hero!

First published in Great Britain by HarperCollins Publishers Ltd in 2002
ISBN-13: 978 0 00 778261 1
ISBN-10: 0 00 778261 6

Text and illustrations copyright © Nick Butterworth 2002
The author asserts the moral right to be identified as the author of the work.

Visit our website at: www.harpercollinschildrensbooks.co.uk

Printed and bound in Belgium

MY FRIENDS
THE RABBITS

Rabbits will play games all day long. They seem to have so much energy! If you were going to organise a picnic with games, the rabbits would be the first in line to join in. (Actually, you might find the fox first in line. You know, because of the picnic part.)

Some of the rabbits are not . . . how can I put it . . . great thinkers. But they are great company and I know at least one little rabbit who is as bright as a button.

Then again, I can think of one who definitely isn't. Still, he spends a lot of his time asleep. And that's alright when you're getting on a bit. Do you know, I could enjoy a nap myself right now . . .

If I wanted to find rabbits,
I think the first place I
would look would be the
playground.

They do enjoy the slide
and the seesaw. And they
always seem to be the last ones to
get dizzy on the roundabout.

Most of them love the swings as well.
All except for one little chap who had, what
the owl called, an 'unfortunate experience'.

The badger had just taught him how to
get the swing to go higher without being
pushed. He was very pleased with himself.

Higher and higher he went. He was
having great fun. It was such a pity
he didn't remember what
he'd been taught about
holding on tight.

THE RABBITS REALLY LIKE . . .

Cold vegetable soup! I found that out
one day when I let my hot soup go cold.
They 'helped me out' as they put it.

Sunset. There's just something about that
time of day that the rabbits love.

THE RABBITS DON'T LIKE . . .

Being picked up by their ears!
(Conjurers please take note!)

Doing sums. Not even easy ones. A rabbit once
told me he thought one plus one equalled
twenty-seven!

You might be surprised to
know that the rabbits like
to play scary games. Just as
long as there's really nothing
to be scared of!

One night, I came across these six rabbits
playing at being ghosts. The yellow ghost
couldn't find a white cloth so she had to use
a duster instead.

Just a moment. . . did I say six rabbits?
It looks as if someone else has joined in
the game too. Perhaps it's the hedgehog.
No, it can't be. He doesn't like
scary games. It must be a
squirrel. Unless, of course,
it really is a . . .

I've got lots of pictures in my photo album.

Did you lose a school tie? Look who found one!

Is this the longest rabbit in the world?

Here are some I took of my good friends, the rabbits.

It can be
very risky
to hold three
balloons if
you're not
very heavy!

'Aaah!'
is for
rabbit.

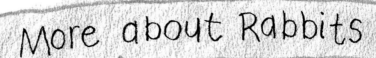

More about Rabbits

You probably know that rabbits like to play Leap-Frog. Did you know that Frogs play the same game and call it Rabbit-Hop?

5

When one of my rabbit friends was a bit poorly he didn't feel like joining in with the others in their running and jumping games. So we decided to make a special book all about rabbits.

Q What is the difference between a rabbit and a hare?

A You'll always see a rabbit covered in hairs, but you'll never see a hare covered in rabbits!

Rabbits can run very quickly. If a rabbit was as big as a horse it could run at 500 kilometres per hour! ZOOM!

12

We really enjoyed doing it and by the time he went home he was feeling much better. It's funny how that can happen.

Here are two pages from our book. Pages five and twelve. I'm not quite sure how they came to be next to each other.

RACING RABBITS

Whenever I watch the rabbits race,
(You'll think I'm daft, I know)
I sometimes get this mad idea,
I'd like to have a go!

Can you imagine what they'd say?
Can you imagine their faces?
"It's Percy!" they'd chuckle and laugh out loud,
"He wants to join our races!"

I know if I raced the rabbits,
I'd lose, but I don't mind.
If we were to have a wheelbarrow race,
I'd leave them all behind!

FAVOURITE PLACES

I collect watering cans. Yes, I know it sounds peculiar, but it's true! I've got lots. Big fat ones, tall thin ones, some with funny handles, some with even funnier spouts.

I keep them in my potting shed, and on a rainy afternoon, that is where you will find the rabbits. They like watering cans too!

The rabbits play a game which is a bit like hide-and-seek, only it's called hide-and-*speak*.

When the others are not looking, a rabbit will hide in one of the watering cans.

The hiding rabbit then has to say something
and the others have to guess which watering
can the rabbit is in.

It can be tricky. The rabbits disguise their
voices and the empty watering cans make
their voices sound strange so that it's hard to
tell where a voice is coming from.

The rabbits play all sorts of other games in
the potting shed too. When the weather is
very bad they almost live there!

They don't really live there, of course. They
live amongst the roots of the big tree house.
That is the rabbits' real favourite place.

Here they are, my friends the rabbits, playing leapfrog. I wonder if that frog sitting on the stump would like to join in. Be careful, little rabbit. Don't leap too far. You'll end up in the water!